P9-CNC-361

Gran
Grandville Public Schools

PURCHASED WITH
BOOK FAIR FUNDS

Mary Marony
Mummy Girl

Grand View Media Center
Grandville Public Schools

Suzy Kline

Mary Marony
Mummy Girl

Illustrations by Blanche Sims

G. P. PUTNAM'S SONS

NEW YORK

Acknowledgments

Special appreciation for their help
with this manuscript to
My editor, Anne O'Connell
My husband, Rufus
My mother, Martha Weaver
and
Chef Scott Richard Kushman

Text copyright © 1994 by Suzy Kline
Illustrations copyright © 1994 by Blanche Sims
All rights reserved. This book, or parts thereof,
may not be reproduced in any form without
permission in writing from the publisher.
G. P. Putnam's Sons, a division of
The Putnam & Grosset Group,
200 Madison Avenue, New York, NY 10016.
G. P. Putnam's Sons, Reg. U.S. Pat. & Tm. Off.
Published simultaneously in Canada.
Printed in the United States of America
Book designed by Colleen Flis and Donna Mark
Text set in Sabon.
Library of Congress Cataloging-in-Publication Data
Kline, Suzy. Mary Marony, mummy girl / Suzy Kline;
illustrated by Blanche Sims. p.   cm.
Summary: Second-grader Mary Marony wants to be
something scary for Halloween so she can get back
at Marvin, who makes fun of Mary's stuttering.
[1. Stuttering—Fiction.   2. Halloween—Fiction.
3. Schools—Fiction.]   I. Sims, Blanche, ill.   II. Title
PZ7.K679Mau 1994 [E]—dc20 93-14348   CIP   AC
ISBN 0-399-22609-5
5 7 9 10 8 6 4

To my daughter

Jen Kline

I love you *and your spirit*

Contents

1

How It All Started

Mary sat down at the table. "Mmmm, cake for breakfast!"

"Torte," Mrs. Marony said. "How does it taste? I have to add some nuts."

Mr. Marony looked up from his crossword puzzle. "I'm glad you got that scholarship to cooking school and could leave that boring factory job. But don't you think dessert for breakfast is a bit much?"

Mrs. Marony grabbed her knife and started chopping walnuts on the bread-board.

"I am going to be a great chef."

Chop, chop.

"In order to be a great chef, I have to take two weeks of baking . . ."

Chop, chop, chop.

". . . two weeks of pastry, two weeks of meat cutting, AND practice at home!"

CHOP, CHOP, CHOP!

Mr. Marony started eating the gooey cake. "I never argue with a woman holding a knife. Just look what happened to the three blind mice."

"They lost their tails to the farmer's wife," Mary said. She loved nursery rhymes.

Mrs. Marony sprinkled some nuts over Mr. Marony's torte. "Thank you, Matthew, for your support."

Ten minutes later, Mrs. Marony left for cooking school, and Mary watched her father do the daily crossword puzzle.

"Aha! 'Predicament' . . . it fits!"

Mary looked at the long word. " 'Predicament'?"

"That's when you get yourself in a jam or a pickle."

Mary giggled. She liked the way her father explained things.

"Now," Mr. Marony said, "I need a five-letter word that means 'a preserved corpse.' "

"A preserved corpse?"

"A dead body that is kept from decaying. Like the Egyptians did."

Mary knew her father was giving her clues and that he probably knew the word already. "Muh-mummy!"

"Right! I always said you were the smartest second-grader in the world."

Then he penciled in the word, M-u-m-m-y.

Mary got up and gave her dad a hug around the neck. He always made her feel good.

"How muh-many houses did you sell this muh-month?" Mary asked. She was proud that her father worked hard in real estate.

Mr. Marony stood up as he looked at the clock. "Not a one, Mary. I didn't sell a house last month either."

Mary grabbed her lunch, book bag, and jacket, and then her father's hand. It was time for them to walk to the bus stop.

"I bet you sell a house today, Dad."

"I'm glad you're optimistic, Mary, but people just aren't buying houses now. Times are hard. We have to count every penny."

Mary had heard her father say that before, but this time he seemed sad when he said it.

When the yellow school bus stopped at the corner, Mr. Marony gave Mary a quick hug goodbye. "Have a good day at school!"

"Love you, Dad," Mary said. Then she hurried onto the bus and grabbed a seat with her two friends, Elizabeth Conway and Audrey Tang.

"I know what I'm going to be for Halloween," Audrey blurted out. "Guess!"

Mary put her book bag between her feet. "Uh . . ."

"A gypsy!" Elizabeth replied.

"How did *you* know?" Audrey asked.

"Because you were a gypsy last year, and the year before that. You love making jewelry!"

Mary fiddled with Audrey's paper-clip necklace. "I love this one."

When the bus stopped at the second corner, and Marvin Higgins got on, Mary made a face. She didn't like Marvin. He was mean to her.

Marvin handed the bus driver a flower.

Mary rolled her eyes. She noticed he still had a handful of flowers left. They were for their teacher, no doubt.

Marvin sat behind the girls. "Ready for the big Halloween school parade on Friday?"

Mary sank down in her seat. She knew she would have to think of something. After Marvin found out Elizabeth and Audrey were going to be a chipmunk and gypsy, he tapped Mary on the shoulder.

"What about Muh-muh-mary Muh-muh-marony?"

Mary folded her arms.

Elizabeth stood up and leaned over the back of the seat. "You shouldn't tease people who stutter. It's mean."

Audrey turned around too. "Besides, Mary doesn't stutter very much any more. Just now and then on M words. Her speech therapist is helping her speak better."

"Sit down, girls!" the bus driver called.

Marvin smiled. He liked it when girls got into trouble.

"Well, what is Muh-mary going to be?" he persisted.

Mary could feel her cheeks getting hot and her face getting red.

"Hmmmm?"

Mary suddenly turned around and talked slowly. "I am going to be something scary. A . . ."

When she realized it started with an M, she stopped. "It . . . it's a secret."

"I bet it won't be as scary as *my* costume!" Marvin bragged.

"I bet it will!" Mary replied.

2

Halloween Ideas

Mrs. Bird put down her book, *Little Witch*. "And so, Madame Snickasnee turned into an anteater, and Moonfire turned out to be Minx's real mother."

Mary smiled. She loved that chapter book.

"Now, boys and girls, I have some exciting news about our town's Halloween art contest."

Everyone sat up.

Marvin stopped drawing bombers in his World War II picture.

"Three children from each class in grades two through four get to paint windows this year on Solano Avenue! The local businesses have whitewashed their windows and donated paint and gift certificates for prizes!"

Marvin flipped a page in his drawing pad and started drawing more bombers.

"The art teacher will decide which three children go from our room. So, start thinking of some good ideas. Remember, it has to have something to do with Halloween. Elizabeth, please pass out paper. Class, start sketching!"

Mary looked at her blank paper. She sat for a long time just thinking.

"I'm done!" Marvin called.

Mrs. Bird looked at the clock. "You've finished in ten minutes?"

Fred Heinz, a boy with big ears, said,
"Marvin's the best artist in the class. He
can draw good and he can draw fast."

"Hmmm," Mrs. Bird said looking at

Marvin's picture. "You have a bunch of fighter planes flying around. What does that have to do with Halloween?"

"Well . . . they're bombers and they're bombing . . ." Marvin quickly looked over at Fred's picture of a pumpkin patch. "Pumpkins! I'll put some pumpkins on the ground right now."

Fred cracked up. "Yeah! It'll be one big orange explosion!"

Mrs. Bird didn't laugh. "Marvin, you draw planes very well, but I don't think the store owners want war scenes on their windows."

Marvin made a face.

"Now, here's a Halloween theme," Mrs. Bird said, holding up Audrey's picture. "Look at this witch. And her black necklace!"

"It's a string of rat tails." Audrey giggled.

23

"How deadly!" Mrs. Bird replied.

Suddenly Mary got an idea.

Half an hour later, Mrs. Bird asked the class to put their names on the back of their pictures before she collected them. "We'll find out who our lucky three winners are after lunch."

Everyone crossed his fingers.

Marvin took one last look at his picture of fighter planes and handed it to the teacher. "Hope my picture doesn't bomb out."

Mrs. Bird rolled her eyes.

That afternoon it was hard to concentrate on math. Right when Mrs. Bird was explaining that, in addition, $7 + 8$ is the same as $8 + 7$, a messenger handed her the winning posters and special permission slips. "Boys and girls," the teacher said, "here are the results!

These three people have been selected to paint store windows tomorrow—Fred Heinz . . ."

Fred jumped out of his chair. "*Yahoo!*"

Marvin put two thumbs up. He knew he would be next.

". . . Giuseppe Rubino . . ."

Everyone knew Giuseppe had made a great haunted house. The class clapped for him.

". . . and . . . Mary Marony."

Elizabeth and Audrey cheered for their friend. Then they frowned. They had wanted to go, too.

Marvin whispered, "You're not the best artist in the class, Muh-mary."

"I know that."

Marvin looked at Mary's poster. "It's not fair you get to go and not me. A mummy band! I can draw instruments better than you. That mummy's horn looks like an Easter lily."

Marvin kept criticizing Mary's drawing. "Look, the mummy playing the xylophone has one arm longer than the other."

Mary gritted her teeth. "Muh-marvin, I happen to know lots about muh-muh-mummmies. I'm going to be a muh-muh-mummy for Halloween!"

Marvin covered his eyes. "I'll believe that when I see it. There are no mummy costumes downtown. I looked them all over."

"I'm muh-muh-making it muh-muh-myself!" Mary hated it when she got upset. She stuttered more.

"Really? How are you going to do it, Mummy Girl?"

Mary took a deep breath, just as her speech therapist had told her to. She was not going to stutter like that again.

Just when Mary was inhaling and exhaling, Mrs. Bird made another announcement. "Now that we have Thursday's window painting settled, I want to talk about Friday's Halloween parade. It will be on the school playground at eleven in the morning. Your parents are invited. The newspaper is coming, and the PTA is serving cider and donuts."

Everyone hooted and clapped except Mary. She was too busy worrying.

She had only two days to make a mummy costume. And it couldn't cost a dime.

3

Mummies and Meat Pie

That night when Mary got home she raced to the bathroom.

Darn! she thought. The Band-Aid can had just three Band-Aids left.

Then she noticed the box of gauze. Perfect!

Mary opened the lid and pulled out the small ball. It was only enough to wrap one hand.

"Dinner!" Mrs. Marony called.

Mary slowly walked back to the kitchen. There was no way she could make a mummy costume.

"What do you think?" Mrs. Marony said, as she set a meat pie on the table.

"It looks nice," Mr. Marony said. "Nice edge."

"I fluted it."

The flute word reminded Mary of her picture. She got up and pulled out the permission slip from her book bag. "I get to paint a window on Solano Avenue tomorrow."

Mr. Marony beamed. "Hey! Maybe you'll get our office window. They just whitewashed it today. You can't see SOLANO AVENUE REAL ESTATE any more. What are you painting, Mary?"

"Here," Mrs. Marony said, serving them each a slice of meat pie. "Is it too runny?"

Mr. Marony shot his wife a look.
"Mary is painting a window tomorrow."

"Great. What about those carrot
chunks? Are they done?"

Mary suddenly felt sad.

She didn't have a costume.

Her mother didn't care about her painting.

And now her dad was angry with her mother.

Mary got up and ran to her room.

"Are the carrots that bad?" Mrs. Marony said.

Mr. Marony shook his head. Then he went and knocked on Mary's door.

"May I come in?"

Mary was sobbing in her pillow.

Mr. Marony slowly opened the door. Then he sat down on her bed. "All your mother can think about right now is being a chef. It won't last much longer. Her big pastry exam is Friday."

Mary sat up and wiped her eyes. Then she leaned on her dad. After a quiet moment, she said, "I'm . . . painting a muh-muh-mummy band. See?" Mary reached for her wrinkled picture.

"I love it! A bunch of corpses making music."

They both laughed.

"I'll look for you on Solano Avenue tomorrow."

Mary smiled. "Parents can come to our school Halloween parade on Friday, too."

"I'll try to come. What are you going to be this year, Mary?"

Mary didn't want to bring up the mummy costume. Her father couldn't afford to buy anything extra right now, and her mother was too busy cooking to help.

Mary got up and walked over to her closet. Way in the back was the formal her mother had gotten her at the thrift store for three dollars last year. "I . . . guess I'll be a fairy princess again like I was at my old school last year. I just need to muh-make another tinfoil wand."

"I can make you one."

"Thanks, Dad." Mary said. But she wasn't smiling. She didn't want to be pretty this year at Halloween. Pretty was boring. She wanted to be something scary and deadly. Like a mummy.

Later that night, her mother tucked her into bed. "Guess what, Princess?"

Mary knew her father had told her mother what she was going to be for Halloween. "What?" She didn't like the nickname Princess.

"Ten more days and I'll be a chef. But I have to study hard, just like you do in school."

Mary nodded. Then she acted sleepy and yawned.

"Goodnight, Princess."

"Goodnight, Mom."

When her mother closed the door, Mary pulled hard on her covers. Ohhh, she was angry!

Then, there was a rrrrrrip. . . .

Mary's big toe had gone through a hole in her white sheet.

Oh, no, she thought. What did I do?

Suddenly, Mary's face brightened.

What a great accident! she thought.

I've got my mummy costume!

4

The Costume

The next morning Mary woke up early.

She tiptoed out of her room and into the kitchen. As soon as she found the big scissors, she tiptoed back to her room.

Mary didn't feel guilty about cutting the sheet. After all, it was ripped already.

Snip.

Mary cut the top of her sheet.

Rrrrrrrip. She ripped the first strip.

Snip.

She cut the second slit.

Rrrrrrrrip. She pulled the piece of sheet all the way to the end.

Two strips done.

Snip.

Rrrrrrrrip.

Snip.

Rrrrrrrrip.

Five minutes later, Mary had twenty long strips of a white sheet. Perfect for her mummy costume tomorrow.

Mary hid the strips in her bottom drawer, where she kept her summer clothes and hardly opened any more. Then she walked over to the linen closet for another flat sheet.

It would be fun to surprise her parents with her mummy costume. She had made it herself and it didn't cost a penny. Wouldn't they be proud of her!

Mary looked at the small stack of fresh towels, dish towels, two pillow cases, and three washcloths. Her mother's sewing basket was on the top shelf. Where were the extra sheets? The laundry!

"Mary!" her mother called from the kitchen. "Want to help me make cinnamon wheels? I have extra pie dough."

"Be there in a minute, Mom!"

After Mary got dressed, she made a sign in bright red crayon that said, DO NOT ENTER. Then she closed her door and taped it onto the knob.

I hope that extra sheet is in the dryer and *not* the washer, she thought.

Mary raced into the kitchen. Her mother was rolling dough on the breadboard. Mary put her arms around her mother's stomach and gave her a squeeze.

"Morning, Mary. I'd hug you back, but I'll get flour all over you."

Mary looked at her mother's hands. They were white and gooey. A round piece of dough was rolled smooth on the breadboard.

"Okay, Mary. Your turn. Spread some butter on the dough and sprinkle it with cinnamon and sugar. Then we'll cut strips and roll them up."

Mary put on an apron and started working. She loved baking with her mother.

As soon as they rolled up the last cinnamon wheel and popped the cookie tray into the oven, Mary snooped in the laundry room around the corner.

Slowly, she lifted the lid of the washing machine. Please don't be here, Mary thought.

Yahoo! It was empty!

Mary glanced in the laundry basket. That was empty too.

She looked inside the big sink.

Empty.

Then she opened the door of the dryer.

It was full!

Mary peeked around the corner. Her parents were sipping coffee at the table and reading. "Do you want me to fold the clean clothes for you?" she asked.

Mr. Marony looked up from his

crossword puzzle. "You're folding clothes? Call the newspaper!"

Mrs. Marony chuckled.

Mary was too serious to laugh. She was looking for something big and white in the dryer.

What's this?

Mary held it up.

Her father's boxer shorts!

Quickly she folded them and reached for something else white. This was big. Her arms stretched wide to hold it up.

A tablecloth!

The rest was odds and ends. Mary shook her head as she folded towels, underwear, and socks. Many had been mended with tiny stitches.

There was no extra sheet.

Suddenly, Mary felt awful.

Her family *was* counting pennies. Her dad hadn't sold a house in months. No wonder they couldn't afford extra sheets right now. They had to keep mending their raggedy ones until her mother became a chef.

"Mary! The cinnamon wheels are hot out of the oven. Come and have some with milk."

"Coming, Mom." Mary closed the dryer door. What a predicament. She would have to keep her cut-up sheet a secret for a while longer. The timing wasn't right.

Mary raced by the kitchen table.

"Aren't you eating?" her mother called.

"I forgot to make my bed."

Mr. Marony got up and went to the phone. *"I'm calling the papers!"*

Mary was not in the mood to laugh about anything. She just dashed into her room and threw the blanket over her one sheet. Then carefully, she smoothed the blanket and added the bedspread. As an afterthought, she tried to tuck the spread under her pillow the way her mother did. There. It looked just like a Tootsie Roll.

Slowly, Mary walked back to the kitchen. Yes, she would keep her secret for a little while longer. But then what? How was she going to replace her old sheet?

5

Windows and Desks

That morning, Mary, Fred, and Giuseppe walked to Solano Avenue with the group of other schoolchildren who were painting windows. Some PTA members and Mr. Fries, the principal, went along as chaperones.

"Do you have an old white sheet?" Mary asked Fred.

"Why? You don't want to get paint on the sidewalk?"

"No."

"You want to be a ghost tomorrow?"

"Maybe." Mary hadn't had much luck asking Audrey and Elizabeth on the bus. They didn't have one white sheet in the house. Just ones with flowers, stripes, cats, and sheep.

"I have one you can borrow. But it's got Bozo the Clown on it."

"No thanks, Fred," Mary said. She was glad when she got to her store window. She wanted to get her mind off the subject of sheets for a while.

"Lucky you," Fred moaned. "You get to paint on an ice cream store. I get a boring insurance office."

"Office windows are just as good," Mary snapped. "They have whitewash on them, too."

"Mary!" a voice called.

When she turned around, she saw her

father across the street down by the corner.

"Hi, Dad!" Mary called back. She could see a fourth-grader painting a huge Count Dracula on her father's real estate window. Even his white fangs!

Fred started painting his pumpkin patch on the window. "I'll probably be here all night. I've got a hundred pumpkins to paint."

Mary picked up her yellow paintbrush and started painting the mummies. She liked putting in the little black beady eyes.

One of the fourth-grade girls was painting on the other side of Mary. "Can I borrow some of your black?"

"Sure," Mary said sliding the pail over to the tall girl.

Mary liked the girl's window. It was Frankenstein reading a book.

"What's the name of the book?" Mary asked.

"Hmmmm," the girl said. "I never thought about that. It *should* have a name. What about . . . *How to Sew?* Frankenstein has so many stitches in his body!"

Mary laughed.

"Do you have a name for your band?"

Mary stepped back. "*I* didn't think about *that.* Let's see . . . Muh-mummy Muh-music?"

"That's fun!" the girl replied.

By noontime, Solano Avenue had dozens of painted windows. Mary liked hers. She had tried to make the horn look like a horn and not an Easter lily.

When they got back to class, everyone was cleaning desks.

"Welcome back!" Mrs. Bird said.

51

"It's fall, so we're turning over a new leaf. Getting rid of the mess, cleaning our desk, and starting fresh!"

Mary smiled. She liked it when her teacher tried to make things rhyme.

Mary knew her desk was a mess, so she started emptying it.

Marvin looked over at her collection of stuff. It made him curious. "You still have Fred's birthday cupcake?"

Mary ignored Marvin. Didn't he know that creative minds have messy desks? That's what the cube on her teacher's desk said.

Marvin dragged the garbage can over to Mary. "Here, I'll help you." Then he pulled a brown bag out of Mary's desk. "What's in here?"

"Take a look, nosy." Mary grinned.

Marvin did.

"Ewee. It's black and hairy."

Mary didn't say anything.

Marvin reached inside and held something up. "A dead bird! Aaaauuugh!" And he jumped two feet in the air.

Everyone stopped what he was doing.

Mrs. Bird came running over. "A what?"

Mary held it up. "It's just an old moldy banana from the first week of school."

Everyone laughed.

Even Mrs. Bird.

Marvin turned pink with embarrassment as Mary dropped the banana into the garbage can. After everyone else returned to their desks, Marvin whispered, "Wait till tomorrow when I come to school in my costume. We'll see who gets scared then."

"We'll see." Mary grinned. She loved the challenge.

Just then a voice came over the intercom and the class became quiet. It was the mayor. After she thanked lots of people, she announced the winners of the Halloween Art Contest.

"The Grand prize of a twenty-five-dollar gift certificate from Tommy's Bike Shop goes to . . . Nimrod Hassawash for his 'Pumpkin Man.' Second place and a ten-dollar ice cream cake from Ice Cream Sam's goes to . . . Javon Brown for his 'Headless Horseman.' "

No one in Mary's class recognized the names of the first- and second-prize winners. They were probably fourth-graders, Mary thought.

"Third prize and a five-dollar gift certificate at Gooberman's Department Store goes to . . . Mary Marony for her 'Mummy Music.' "

Mrs. Bird's class burst out cheering.

Except for Marvin. He made a face. "You think you're so clever, Mary. Just wait until tomorrow."

Mary ignored him and ran over to Elizabeth and Audrey. The girls jumped up and down as they made a huddle.

"What are you going to spend your certificate on?" Mrs. Bird asked.

"Magic Markers?" Audrey asked.

"A book?" Elizabeth asked.

"A new sheet!" Mary exclaimed.

6

Mummy Girl

Friday morning, Mrs. Marony got up from the breakfast table. "Well, it's P Day!"

"P Day?" Mr. Marony took another sip of coffee. "What's that?"

"Time for my Pastry exam, and for Mary to put on her Princess costume."

Mr. Marony chuckled.

Mary made a polite smile. She knew it wouldn't be long now before she could tell her mother *everything*. "Good luck on your exam, Mom." Then she ran to her room, closed the door, and waited for her mother to leave the house.

Mary put her ear next to the door and listened. Her parents talked for a minute, and then there was the sound of the front door. It was opened and then closed.

She was gone!

Mary turned, got out her long winter underwear, and put it on. Then she started winding a strip of sheet around her leg. It wasn't easy.

When there was a knock on the door, she knew the time had come to tell her father. She needed his help. How angry could he be? After all, Mary thought, she had gotten her mummy idea from him.

"Come on in, Dad."

"Mary?"

"Muh-mom!" Quickly Mary hopped into bed and pulled up the covers.

"I have a few minutes. Need some help with your dress?" Mrs. Marony called.

When there was no answer, Mrs. Marony opened the door and looked at Mary. "Why are you in bed?"

"I'm not feeling so well."

"Want to talk about it?"

Mary didn't say anything. She just started to quiver. Why didn't her mother just leave? Go take your test, Mary wished.

But instead Mrs. Marony went around to the other side of the bed and got under the covers too. Clothes, shoes, and all.

"Mary," she said, "when I got in the car, I started feeling guilty. I had forgotten to say goodbye and wish you a happy day."

Mary felt a warm tear roll down her cheek.

She couldn't hold the truth back any longer.

But just when she was about to tell her mother everything, Mrs. Marony threw back the covers. "What happened to your top sheet? And why are you in long underwear?"

Mary slowly got out of bed and walked over to her bottom drawer. "It's here," she said, holding up twenty long strips of cloth.

Mrs. Marony sat up and smoothed her hair. "You . . . cut up your sheet?"

Mary took a deep breath. "Yesterday, when I accidently ripped it, it seemed like a good idea for a muh-mummy cos-tume."

"You want to be a mummy?"

"I did. Now, it . . . doesn't seem like such a good idea."

Mrs. Marony placed her hands on her daughter's shoulders. "So this is why you're not feeling well?"

Mary nodded. Then she sobbed. "I'm sorry, Muh-muh-mom. I was going to tell you when your test was over."

Mr. Marony knocked on the door. "Everything okay in there?"

"Fine!" Mrs. Marony called. "We're working on Mary's costume."

Mary wiped her eyes. "We are?"

Mrs. Marony gave Mary a long hug. Then she picked up the first strip of cloth and started winding it around Mary's leg. "Yes, but your dad is not going to be happy about having to buy another sheet. I could have mended the rip."

Mary reached for the Gooberman's gift certificate on her dresser. "This is to help pay for a new one."

"Your prize for third place?"

"Uh-huh."

Now Mrs. Marony got tears in her eyes. "I sure love you, Mummy Girl. I don't think you'll cut up things again without permission."

Mary held up two fingers. "No, Mom. Brownie's honor."

Mary watched her mother wrap the long strips of cloth around her legs, arms, stomach, chest, and neck. Each time she came to the end of a strip, she tied on a new one. When she came to Mary's face, she left openings for her eyes, nose, and mouth.

"Now you look like you just escaped from an Egyptian museum!" Mrs. Marony said.

Mary walked around her room and dangled her arms like a stiff mummy. She loved her finished costume!

"Wait until Marvin sees me. I'll really scare him. He thinks he's going to scare muh-me."

"You care about Marvin now?"

"No! I hate him."

Mrs. Marony raised her eyebrows.

Mr. Marony knocked on the door again. "The bus is going to be here any minute now."

"We're ready!" Mrs. Marony sang out. "Come and see the fairy princess."

Mary giggled. This was fun. "Okay, Daddy! Open the door but close your eyes first."

"Here I come!"

When the door swung open, Mr. Marony's eyes were tightly shut. He was also holding something in his hand.

"When can I give the most beautiful daughter in the world her magic tinfoil wand?"

"Now," Mary giggled.

Mr. Marony opened his eyes. "Aaaaughhhhhh! A dead corpse!"

Mary jumped up and down giggling. "You fooled me, Mummy Girl!"

Mary grabbed her lunch and book bag. "Wait until I fool the kids at school. Especially Muh-marvin!"

7

The Parade

When Mary got inside the bus, all the boys and girls stopped talking and stared. *Who* was this mummy? everyone wondered.

It was easy for Mary to spot her two friends in the busload of costumed children. She just looked for the gypsy and the chipmunk.

"It's *me, Mary*," she said.

"Ohhhhhhhhhhh!" Audrey shivered.

"You could have fooled me!" Elizabeth replied.

Mary giggled as she waited eagerly for Marvin's stop. "Wait till he sees me!"

When they came to the second corner, Mary watched each costumed person get on.

A TV set, cat, cowgirl, and pirate. Marvin wasn't one of them.

"He probably got a ride to school," Mary said. "I'll see him in class."

As soon as the girls got into the classroom, they went to their seats.

Mrs. Bird showed up as a witch in a black cape and hat, with green makeup. She also had two raisins on her chin for warts.

"Happy Halloween, class!"

69

"Madame Snickasnee!" the class exclaimed. That was their favorite witch's name.

That morning the children went to the auditorium for a special program. A man and a woman played their guitars, sang songs, and told stories. They also reminded the children to have their parents check their candy and to trick-or-treat at the houses where they knew the people.

When it was time to line up for the playground parade, Mary kept looking for Marvin. Was he sick? Mary was surprised she was so disappointed. A Halloween parade just seemed more fun with Marvin around. She really wanted him to see her in her mummy outfit.

As they marched out into the playground, Mary noticed a car pull into the parking lot. A big hairy lion jumped out of the car and roared. When he ran over to their line, Mary knew who it was.

"Marvin!" everyone yelled.

Marvin leaped in the air as he roared, "RRRRrrrr! This was my brother's costume in *The Wizard of Oz!*"

When he got in line, he noticed Mary right away. "Hey, Mummy Girl!" And he clawed at the air.

Mary held up her bandaged arms and moaned, "Where . . . were . . . yoooooooooooooooooooo?"

"At the dentist. You look pretty deadly, Mummy Girl." Then Marvin changed the subject. "I just saw your parents pull into the parking lot."

Mary stopped oooohing. "You did?"

She looked over at the large group of parents. Her mother was wearing a chef's hat and long white apron. Her dad was waving a package.

"Hi, Mom! Hi, Dad!" Mary waved back.

Mr. Marony called out, "Just picked up one flat sheet on sale at Gooberman's for $4.99. You're paid in full."

"Yippee!" Mary replied. Then she asked, "How was your exam, Mom?"

"Good, but I'm not finished yet. I'm just taking a quick mummy break!"

Mary smiled as she crossed her bandaged fingers. "Good luck, Mom!"

Just then the newspaper reporter came around calling the names of the Halloween window art winners. "I want to take your picture."

Mary, Nimrod, and Javon stood together and smiled.

Click.

"Now," the reporter said, "each of you pick two scary people for a second picture."

Audrey and Elizabeth jumped up and down. "Mary!" They wanted her to pick them.

Mary looked over at Marvin. He wasn't roaring any more. He knew he wouldn't be picked.

Mary looked back again at her two friends, the gypsy and the chipmunk.

They were cute but they were not very scary.

Mary walked stiffly over to the fourth grade and picked the girl who painted next to her window. She was a scary Frankenstein.

"Where's your sewing book?" Mary teased.

The girl laughed. "I was happy you won. Thanks for picking me for the newspaper picture."

"You helped muh-me win. I named my picture Muh-mummy Muh-music because of you, remember?"

"One more," the photographer called to Mary.

Mary looked back at her class and the sea of waving hands. "Me! Me!" everyone called.

Slowly she walked over to Marvin and grabbed his tail. "Come on, Lion! You're scary enough for the newspaper."

"Me? You picked me? I don't believe it!"

"Yes, you, Muh-marvin."

Marvin immediately jumped up and clawed at the photographer. "RRRrrr!" he shouted.

Then he whispered, "Thanks, Mary. You're one *grrrrrrrrrrrrr . . . great* mummy!"

Mary smiled.

It was the first time Marvin didn't call her Muh-muh-mary. And it was the first time he actually said something nice to her.

Mary liked that.

She knew she would remember Halloween in second grade.

It was the first time she didn't hate Marvin.